I0713276

Sandy

Cereal at Midnight

by

Sandra Gail Fontana

Illustrated by her Dad

William Fontana Sr.

US Copyright 2015 TXu 1-963-279

ISBN   978-0-9859599-7-5

Acknowledgement:

Barbara Minor has worked very hard to correct s Sandy's spelling and grammatical errors. Will Fontana has made some very helpful suggestions for art display and has made the cover design for this book. Michael Gage Sandy's husband had been very supportive and has carefully saved Sandy's manuscript and supported its illustration and publication.

Introduction:

These delightful, humorous, and sometimes sad stories were written by my daughter Sandy when she was twelve to thirteen years old (circa 1982). Sandy died tragically at the age of 36 (2006). I know she would be happy to know that in spite of the demons that tortured her, her childhood short stories have survived to tickle and inspire.

There is a saying that the good die young, and that was certainly the case with my daughter Sandy. She had a delightful sense of humor and a bright, creative mind. I have illustrated her stories, and in a way, it has brought her back to me and I hope, to you, as well.

Sandy had a unique gift that made it possible for her to consciously tap into the part of her mind that created her night-time dreams, thus the title "Cereal at Midnight." Therefore, I call these stories "surreal short stories" because they come from the place where dreams are made; *they are, indeed, "Cereal at Midnight."*

Table of Contents

Cereal at Midnight

Alone, in the cold distance stood the lonely CHEX CEREAL BOX, cereal flowing out of the forgotten box.

The colorful flowered tablecloth was spinning, spinning out to clouds of rainbow space.

Away, on the shores of the sea and seashells,

mermaids laughed as they watched the moon fall.

Drops of milk dripped and dribbled out the sides of fish and frogs' mouths as they savored the delicious Chex cereal on the wild island of Gaboooooooooooooooooooooooooooooooooooki.

The Pink Country

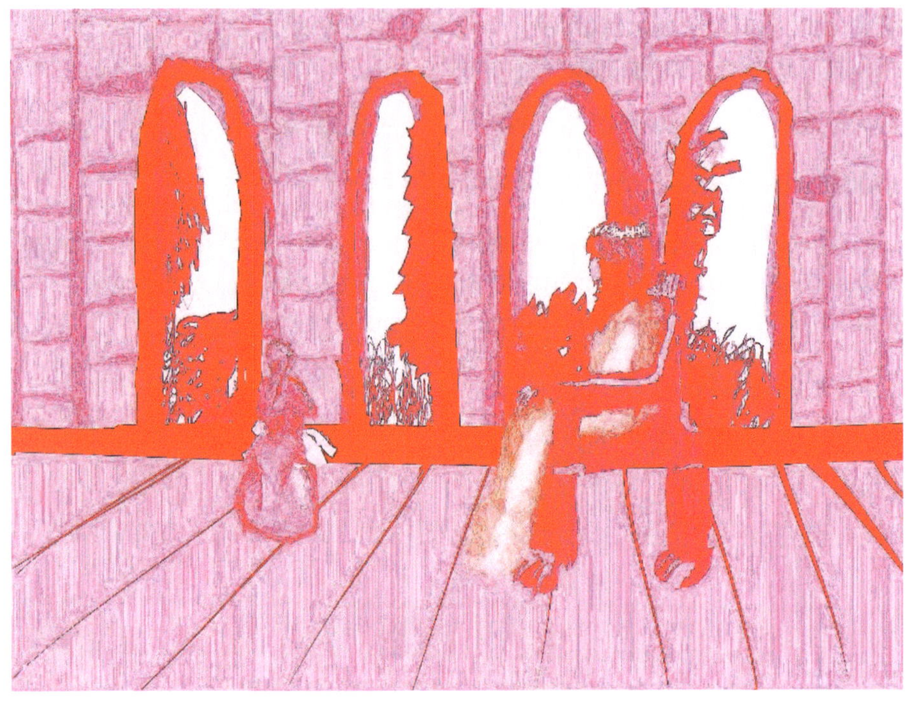

Once upon a time, there was a queen who loved the color pink. So she decided to make the whole country pink. She even made the people of the country wear all pink clothes and paint the grass, trees and everything pink, even their hair. The queen had twelve daughters. The youngest daughter was two years old, and as she got older, she got very sick of pink.

She liked blue, yellow, green, and purple. She liked almost every color except pink. When she turned 18, she traveled around the country. One day, she came home wearing a rainbow shirt with blue and purple pants.

She washed the color pink out of her hair. When the queen saw her daughter, she was shocked. She got mad! But soon the country realized how pretty she was even though she didn't wear pink.

The eleven other daughters started to wear colored clothes, and so did the whole country. Then they began to change the color of their clothes to natural colors. The queen was now happy with her daughter for being unique. The queen realized she was bored with pink anyway.

Why Fish Can't Breathe Air

A long time before man, fish could breathe air, and could walk on land. Later on, man came along, and the fish were so frightened that they went into the water and waited for man to leave. The fish waited for days, weeks, and months.

The fish started to lose their legs. Pretty soon their legs were gone because they didn't use them.

One day a fish was getting chased around the once quiet stream. It was caught and eaten by the people. *Soon the fish were being chased all of the time.*

When the fish found out they couldn't breathe the air anymore, they were mad. They know now they're water animals only, *but they still wait for us to leave.*

The Girl Who Didn't Do Her Homework

One day in a freezing classroom, Candy was sitting down, daydreaming, and not listening to the assignment, but she didn't care anyway. Her parents were away on vacation, so she didn't even do her homework.

Finally, she couldn't get in her room anymore because of all the stacked homework. Every day her amount of undone homework increased. It was starting to fill the whole house. The house was so packed with it she couldn't get in. *It started coming out of the chimney and, eventually scattered all over California!*

When she got suspended from school for a month, she remembered that her parents were going to return home in four weeks. So she started on the 1979's homework. She stayed up night and day for two weeks. She got up to the 1980's homework. Every day she turned in homework after school was out. She only had a week left to do the rest, *so everybody helped her because they wanted California cleaned up!*

She was so glad when the homework was finished and turned in. So were the people who lived in California. Her mom was glad her room was clean. *Now Candy always does her homework!*

The Beautiful Bluebird

One summer morning, four bluebirds were born in the backyard of a very wealthy family. The family had a dog named Dusty. The mother bird wanted to leave because the dog might hurt her babies. So the father bird made wings with leaves, paper, and stuff in the backyard and set them on the nest. Somehow the wings started working, and the nest flew out of the tree. But when they were almost out of the backyard, one baby fell out. The mother said, "Keep on going. That baby isn't as cute as the others."

Dusty saw the bird, and before he saw its sad eyes, he almost ate it. Dusty brought the bird to the little girl who was his owner. The girl saw the broken-winged bird and brought it to the veterinarian. The veterinarian put a cast on it and told her to take good care of it. Dusty and the girl liked the bird.

Every day the bird became more beautiful. When the girl took the cast off the bird, she said that she was going to miss it, and she could already see Dusty was going to also. But to her surprise, when she let the bird go, it didn't leave. It just flew around the big backyard and stayed with them. Sometimes the beautiful bird would leave, but it always came back. *The bluebird was way prettier than its two brothers and one sister.*

The Girl Who Had to Write a Theme

One day a girl had to write a theme. She had all week to do it, but she couldn't think of a topic.

When she finally wrote one at the last minute, it was very bad. She got an "F" on it. She knew that she needed to do better. She needed more time to do it.

So every Monday night, with one button, she turned off all clocks in all of the world, *and from then on she got B's and A's.*

Craderface and His Family

Once, a long time ago, there were moonlings. Moonlings were creatures that look just like earthlings, but they lived on the moon. Craderface was a moonling boy, and he had a family, a sister, baby brother, and mom and dad.

I don't know how it happened, but all of the moonlings died except Craderface and his family, and they got really bored and sad after all the other moonlings were dead. So Craderface went to Earth on his meteor vehicle.

He saw creatures on Earth that looked and talked just the same as he did. He went back to tell his family. When his dad and mom heard, they were glad. So they packed and left to go to the Earth. When they landed, they found out that what Craderface had said about Earth was true. The family now just never tells anybody that they are moonlings. Nobody knows who are moonlings and who are earthlings. *The moonlings might take over someday because their family is very big!*

The Golden and Silver Unicorns

A long time ago when towns and countries had different names, there was a country called Golden Country. It really wasn't golden it just had a girl unicorn that was very special because she was a golden unicorn.

Another country was called Silver Country. Of course there was a silver boy unicorn in that country.

The two countries were enemies. They were at war all of the time until the day the two unicorns met. They liked each other a lot, and so they ran away and got married. The countries were furious with anger.

Then one man thought that if the two unicorns from enemy countries which hated each other could get along so well then the two countries should be able to get along too. So they all got together and had a big party to honor the wedding. *After that, the Golden and Silver countries got along great!* They lived happily ever after.

The Foolish Butterfly

One sunny day, a beautiful butterfly was born. Every butterfly in the whole town came to see her. They brought her presents, gold, and silver, because she was so beautiful. When she got older, she was very conceited.

Other butterflies would do all her work for her, and if any butterfly was in her way, they would always move. This went on for a long time.

One day when she was playing in a lady's garden, the lady of the garden saw her. The lady collected butterflies. When the lady got in the butterfly's way, the beautiful butterfly expected her to move, but she didn't. Instead, she caught the beautiful butterfly with a net.

None of the other butterflies helped her because she was so mean to them. Luckily, the butterfly managed to escape, and after that, the foolish butterfly realized that because she was so conceited, she wasn't truly beautiful, *and she became loving and kind.*

Jessica's Missing Daughter

One night, in the middle of a terrible thunderstorm, a lady named Jessica was walking in the driveway of a store when she saw people screaming and running from some kind of ugly creature. It was too dark to see it at first.

Then

the creature came closer, and she could see how repulsive it was. She jumped in her car and drove away as fast as she could. When she looked in her rearview mirror, she saw it again. It was Mr. Hyde!! Mr. Hyde was all hairy, and he was chasing her car.

When she reached home, she got out of her car and tried feverishly to get in her house. She couldn't find her keys in the darkness. She knew the only way to get in the house without the key was to go through the transom above the door. She saw the next door neighbor's ladder and used it to get up to the transom.

She opened the transom she gingerly climbed into her house.

Mr. Hyde was still after her. When she was in her house, she went upstairs to call the police. The phone was dead. Jessica then went down stairs to see if her daughter was alright. *Her daughter was gone!*

She was flustered, irritated, and sad. She hated that vicious Mr. Hyde. Jessica babbled to herself for a while and then decided to go to the My Devil Kingdom where she was almost sure her daughter was being held prisoner.

With her mournful eyes, she saw an Osprey fly over a plume of smoke. The sight sent a shiver down her back as

she hunched down, trying to think of a way to get to the kingdom
and bring her daughter back.

She found a boat and sailed it across the ocean.

The atmosphere was freezing, and Jessica worried that another storm would hit.

Miraculously, she found the My Devil Kingdom after a week of searching.

When the boat reached the shallows, after so much time in the seat of the boat, she seemed welded to it when she tried to get out. However, she managed to climb out and headed in the direction of the castle.

She went up to the guards of the My Devil Kingdom and told them that she was related to Dr. Jekyll, so they let her in a room. She saw Dr. Jekyll drink something, and it made him turn into Mr. Hyde. It was incredible. He got all hairy.

He didn't know that she saw him. She crept out of the room and searched for her daughter! When she saw a dungeon, she thought that her daughter might be in there.

She heard a voice calling to her from inside the dungeon. She looked in and could see her daughter in a cell with rusty bars. They were so rusty that Jessica could just pull them out of the wall to set her daughter free.

The guards came, and the mother and daughter ran for their lives. *When they made it to the boat, the thunderstorm stopped and*

 They escaped and lived happily ever after.

The Shower of Colors

One dark night a girl was coloring.

Suddenly, her crayons, paint, and all the colorful things in the
world turned black and white,

like a black and white T.V. It was very weird. Things looked boring. She hated it that way! But everybody thought she was weird because she was the only one to see things that way.

She saw everything in black and white until one day, she saw a cloud that had all the colors that she had ever seen in her life.

She started to hear thunder and lightning, and soon it started to rain hard. The rain wasn't normal.

It had colors in it, and every time one of the drops landed on something, it would return back to its original color.

Everything turned back to its normal color, even inside where no rain had fallen. Then she heard a voice of a creature, or something, saying, *"Color your pictures more colorful, and I'll make things more colorful for you!"*

The Acne Miracle Cure

One day a mean prince was in the cellar of the castle, hard at work ruining his poor brother's invention, a powerful potion to remove pimples. In the process of ruining his brother's work, he became curious. He mixed some of the potion in a bowl and then put it on his own face. An hour later, all of his pimples were gone.

What a discovery! Instead of ruining his poor brother's invention, he sold the potion. Soon, he became very rich from selling the "Acne Miracle Cure."

The wealthy prince would not share any of the money from the sale of the potion with his brother, so the poor brother locked the door to the castle cellar. The rich brother got very angry.

A month went by, and the people who bought the potion wanted their money back because after working for awhile the potion not only stopped working but gave them more pimples than they ever had. They all sued, and the wealthy prince went broke.

The people still wanted a miracle cure for pimples. The poor brother went to work and perfected his own "Acne Miracle Cure."

He became very rich and never gave any of the money from the success of his miracle cure to his brother.

Faeme

Once there was a girl nicknamed Faeme. She liked the name Faeme, but her real name was Elizabeth. There is a good reason the name is so special to her.

Every Monday night, she can't think of a theme to write although it is due every Tuesday.

So, on Tuesdays before class, she goes in the library and sits down and thinks of a theme. Then she writes her theme.

Today she has only five minutes. Do you think she'll make it? Well, she does!

Her nickname became Fast Theme, *but now they just call her Faeme.*

The Unknown Treasure

One day, in a town called Untioch, Sandy and Christy were riding their bicycles all around. They decided to go down to the river and eat lunch, which they brought in a backpack. When they got there, they ate and then they played and rode around.

They had been playing on the rocks and watching people fish when Sandy fell into the water and hit her head very hard on a rock under the water.

Christy looked furiously in the green yucky water for her. Soon she saw Sandy's head bobbing up above the water. Christy jumped in and brought Sandy to shore. She was unconscious.

When Sandy became conscious, she said that she hit her head on a rock and jewels came out of the rock. Christy didn't know Sandy to lie, so she looked under the water, and sure enough, she saw jewels all over the place.

They gathered all the jewels up in the backpack and stuffed them in their pockets and everywhere else they could find to put them in. Because of all they now had to carry, Sandy went to nearby hotel to call her mom and ask for a ride home.

Her mom didn't believe her story until she picked up Christy and Sandy. Sandy's head wasn't injured at all, just a little bump.

They all lived happily ever after because Sandy and Christy gave a lot of money to the needy children and money to help the whales and poor people and to churches and everything. After all of that, they did not have any money left. *They found out that they were just as happy without it.*

The Radio

In a house in New York, there were five teenagers that were criminals. One day they all promised not to steal anything from each other. But the pact didn't seem to work because things continued to be missing. They all got very mad at each other because they thought that one among their group was stealing everything.

This went on for a month. T. V.'s were stolen, shampoo, couches, money. But one night, one of the teenagers got out of bed to spy on the others because he wanted to find out who was doing the stealing. He heard a loud crunching in the living room.

When he went in there, he saw the radio. It had become a radio monster with a giant mouth and was eating up things in the house!

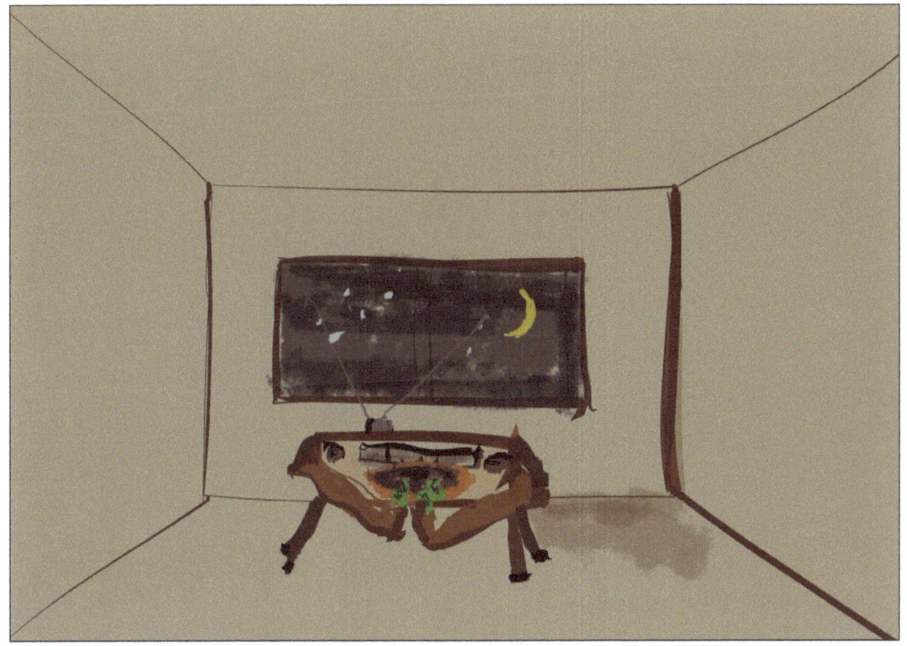

He woke up the others. They could hardly believe their eyes.

They all got together and destroyed the radio and got all the missing things out of it. Then they trusted each other and didn't steal anything again. *Nobody, other than the five teenagers, could ever know how all of this ever happened.*

I Don't Want a White Christmas

One hot December day in Antioch, Laura wished she could have a white Christmas.

On Christmas Eve, Laura bumped her head on the bedpost and got knocked out. *When she regained consciousness, she immediately fell asleep and started dreaming. In her dream, Laura woke up* and slowly walked down the stairs. She couldn't wait to see all of the presents that she got.

When she entered the room where the Christmas tree was, she was surprised.

Everything in the room and the room itself was white. She thought it looked very boring.

Nobody was in the house. She opened her presents, and they were all white. She hated that everything was that way and became so sad.

She heard her mother's voice faintly in the background. *She really woke up this time. She was so happy that it was just a dream.* Laura said, "I don't want a white Christmas!" *She went downstairs and had the best Christmas ever!*

Dandelion, the Swimming Mouse

A mouse named Dandelion lived in a dark and cold corner of the old barn where he was born and raised.

His parents got eaten by a hostile cat named Zap.

Dandelion hated Zap. Zap always tried to kill and eat poor Dandelion. One day, as Dandelion was happily eating a piece of cheese, Zap started to run after him.

Dandelion was trapped! He bit a hole through the old and thin barn wall and got out. He wasn't free yet! Zap got through an open window.

Zap chased Dandelion until Dandelion was trapped again by a pond. Dandelion jumped into the water and found out that he could breathe water like a fish. Zap jumped in and almost drowned.

Zap was very mad, but he never chased Dandelion again, and after that, *Dandelion became known as Dandelion the swimming mouse!*

Skipper and Licorice

In a far-off land where no human has ever been seen, magical things happen. Things are much larger than usual. There are mostly dogs the size of humans.

One day, in the far-off land, a dog had babies, not the usual babies. They were small and tiny. Their mom kicked them out of this land because of how weird and different they were.

The little dogs landed in the United States in my backyard.

They are now my pets and I love them. I named my black one Licorice. He is so cute and playful. The other one is Skipper; he is brown and cute and playful.

Report Fever

One day as a teacher was giving the class a report to do, he started to think of more reports he could give the class to do in the future. He went home that night and thought of millions of gross reports to give his class. The next day he gave the class another report that was due the next week.

Soon the teacher went crazy because he loved giving reports and making kids stay up all night just to finish them. Soon, all of the teachers started to do the same thing as him. *The kids hated it!* So they went on strike, but the principal made them go back to school, and soon the kids were back doing endless reports.

One day all of the kids came to school with purple faces. Every day it got worse. Doctors did not know what to do.

One day it got worse, because all of the kids in the world started to catch it. Then one day, the kids started to get yellow dots on their purple faces.

The next morning when the teacher told the kids he had accidently burned the reports in his fireplace, they were very happy. Their faces turned their normal color. But the teacher's face turned bright red because of his embarrassment.

So the people saw how to cure the kids. They threw away all of the reports in the world. *The teacher's face stayed bright red!*

The Girl with the Yellow Umbrella

"Why do you always carry that stupid yellow umbrella around all the time?" asked Janey to a girl named Holly.

Holly didn't answer.

Janey, Carrie and Cindi always teased her. It was in the middle of the summer.

One day as they were teasing her, gray clouds formed in the sky.
Janey, Carrie and Cindi did not care. They went on teasing her.
It started to rain. Soon it was raining pretty hard. It turned into a
storm. The storm got very bad.

Holly just opened up her umbrella and used it. It started to flood.
So she just turned it upside down and used it as a boat. The girls
were soaked and started to drown.

Holly saved them by letting them get into her umbrella boat.

After that Holly, Janey, Carrie, and Cindi were all very good friends.

The Little Girl and the Big Oak Tree

One hot summer day in a village called Blackberry Village, there was a little girl named Stephanie. She was getting into her car with her family after the moving van left with all the family's belongings. They were all moving to a town called Rainbow Creekside.

When Stephanie started to live at her new house, she couldn't find any friends.

One day she went into her backyard to play. She saw an oak tree. It was very pretty and also big. Stephanie climbed it and loved to play on it. Every day, after that, she went to play on it. She liked it a lot. That made the tree happy and so it started grow bigger.

Months went by and the tree was so happy that it grew bigger and

bigger.

After some years went by, Stephanie's mom and dad said the tree was getting too big and that the roots of the tree were ruining the pipes under their house. They said that they would have to chop the tree down or move.

The tree heard what they said, and it cried tears of sap.

Stephanie too was getting older. When she was 17, they chopped down the beautiful old oak tree. Stephanie was so upset that she decided to move away.

She went into the backyard and looked at the stump of her best friend. The oak tree started to speak.

It said, "Don't be sad, I am still alive, and I will see you at your new house."

She really did not understand what the tree meant. She got married and moved into her new house.

One day she was in her new backyard, thinking of all of the fun she had with the oak tree. And to her surprise, she saw the ground start breaking and a big oak tree came out.

It was her old oak tree. She was so happy.

She heard the phone ring and she ran back inside to get it. It was her parents. They said, *"The roots of the old oak tree kept* growing and grew so big that they tipped our house over!"

A Strange House on the Block

Kelli, Tricia, Michelle, and Christy were all in a club called the "Homework Burners." One day as they were looking through binoculars at people's houses and backyards from their treehouse, they came across a very strange house. It was far away, so they could not see it up close. They decided to get closer to it.

When they were nearer, at first they thought it was haunted. They all decided to scatter and look around it.

Kelli started screaming! All the other girls ran to see what the matter was. They looked around in silence for a few seconds, and then Christy said, "What did you do that for, Kel?"

Almost speechless, Kelli answered, "There's an upside-down lady in that window!"

"How do you figure that?" said Michelle.

"Look for yourself!" cried Kelli.

They all crept around the corner to see. Tricia said, "I don't see any upside-down lady in the window. All I see is a plant with a lot of leaves."

It was a leafy potted plant in the window, put there by the people who were moving in.

Theme Lady

One day a rich man decided to hire a maid. He had hired many already. When he hired her, she turned out to be a good maid, but every night she would sit in a chair silently and write themes.

He was very mean to her. Nobody in the world had ever heard of themes. He locked her in her room every night,

but he was nice to all of the other maids.

She had an imaginative mind. The other maids just thought that she was an ugly and dirty person. For two years, every night she would write her themes. They were wonderful stories, but she did not share them with anyone.

*One night she finished all her themes and put them into a book.
She crept out the window and brought her book to the president.*

*He loved her themes! He made her famous, and from then on,
she was known as the "Theme Lady."*

A Fair Victory in Old Tennis Shoes

One day a family went to a basketball game that their youngest daughter was playing in. She was considered by some to be too small to play.

The family had a friend that was a scientist, and he had invented a lot of things. The scientist wanted the team of the family that he was friendly with to win because the other team was mean, had twice as many players, *and worse of all, they cheated.*

The team he liked always played fair. The scientist decided to invent something to even things out.

Right before the game started, he gave the players on his favorite team new tennis shoes. The players did not have time to ask any questions.   So they just slipped them on and out onto the court they ran.

Suddenly, when the game started, they felt the tennis shoes start moving! It was like they had a mind of their own. The underdogs got the ball, and the crowd was cheering. It was very hard for the girl to make a basket because she was so short. So she jumped! When she jumped, wings popped out of her tennis shoes and flew her up to the basket. She easily threw the basketball in.

The shoes went like rockets to help the team get the ball. The little girl's team was winning until halftime, when the other team ripped the underdogs' shoes right off of their feet.

Now, what were they going to do? Well, they put on their old tennis shoes and started playing. The score was 35 to 0 in favor of the underdogs.

Now they were on their own. When the game was almost over, the score was 40 to 40. The little girl ran up and took the ball from a girl on the other team. *She ran, made the basket and won the game in her old tennis shoes!*

MIN
SEC
Visitor

Freaky Tuesday

Today was very freaky. This morning, while waiting for the bus in the rain, I thought I saw a purple whale with pink dots on it.

I laughed. When I was laughing, my tongue flew out of my mouth

20 inches!

The bus came around the corner over people's lawns. When I got
on the bus, I looked out the window, and the street was a rainbow
that went down like a swirly slide.

We slid down it, and I was having fun and holding on tight to my seat. Kids looked at me like I was strange. When we got to school, it was on a cloud and Mr. Pinion had bare feet!

I was laughing, and when I fell on my knees, I went through the cloud. I landed on grass. It was the schoolyard. I don't know how that happened. I jumped on a unicorn and went to class. I was late. Mr. Hack's hair was curly!

He said, "Why are you late?"

I suddenly couldn't open my mouth. My back turned into an ice cube! He told me to sit down. My back started to run around the room!

At recess I slid across the grass and landed in a mud puddle and saw swans in it!

At lunchtime a turtle tried to attack me!

After school everything was normal like nothing had happened.

"What's new?" Christy said.

I said, "Nothing."

Nobody had noticed anything I saw today. I even said, "Thank you," to a mean boy today! *This may have been a normal day for you but not for me!*

The Great Escape

Thrown in a well by Madam Trocxell, Julie was screaming for

help. Sinking deeper and deeper, she saw a strange tunnel. There was a light coming from it from far away. Julie was shoulder deep in the

mud.
So she climbed into the tunnel, crying as she realized this was her
last hope. She crawled farther and farther into the tunnel toward
the light.

Thirty minutes had gone by and she was still crawling. The light got brighter and brighter as she moved closer to it. The light was also getting bigger and bigger. She got tired and dizzy and dozed off into sleep. When she woke up, she was being carried off on a stretcher by about 1,000,000 tiny yellow, purple, blue, and gold soldiers. They walked 100 miles an hour,

so she didn't dare jump off.

They were singing songs that are popular today and laughing in a high-pitched laugh with their silver teeth sticking out.

She was terrified!

Where was she going?

What were they going to do to her?

Find out next week.

To be continued.

The Great Escape (part 2)

Still terrified, Julie tried desperately to escape. They entered a purple, foggy room. On the other side of the room was a fountain of many colors including pink, yellow, blue, red, and gold.

They tied her up and dragged her to the fountain. She couldn't scream because it seemed impossible, because the fountain was so beautiful and everything was so peaceful.

They threw her in it.

Deeper and deeper she sank into the water. The water was warm, and amazingly, she could breathe under that magical water.

Millions of differently colored birds flew around her and threw sparkly gold glitter all over her which untied the ropes.

She was glad to be free.

The deeper she got, the more her ears hurt. Suddenly a unicorn flew through, or rather swam through, using his wings as fins. He flew underwater through a bunch of silver and gold fish. Then, he swam toward her.

He told her to get onto his back and to hold onto his mane.

She did, and they went through diamond tunnels with tremendous speed. At the end of the tunnel, there was a bubble-like door, and it opened for them.

She was at her house on the farm!

She was so happy to be home. The unicorn lowered one of his wings to the ground and let her climb down.

She turned around to thank it, but it was gone. Julie ran to her home, crying with happiness.

Wheel People

I warn you, stay away from wheel people. They are dangerous.
They roll in the spring and summer mostly. *But still be cautious in winter and fall.*

One sunny day as I was walking home from Christy's house, I saw one. He was strange looking. Suddenly about fifty of them came out of garages. *They were chasing me!*

They have four wheels on their feet. They are scary. I hid behind a bush of flowers. I looked up and saw one flying over me *on a board with wheels.*

They captured me and brought me to a weird room. It was hard to breathe in that room. I couldn't stand up because the floor was really slippery.

I hit my head on a wall. I was unconscious.

When I was conscious again, I was back behind the bush of flowers. The wheel people were gone.   There was no trace of them.

If you ever see them, run! I was lucky!

Where Bubble Gum Comes From

Many years ago on another planet, a creature was chewing on a plant-like thing that they usually chewed on their planet. It was called "guck."   It came in different flavors and colors. We didn't have gum at that time.

One day one of the creatures was chewing some guck, when all of a sudden, its mouth was stuck shut. They couldn't get it open. For weeks it was stuck shut from the sticky guck. Its mouth was practically plastered shut.

Finally, one day it started to open. While it was opening and the creatures were cheering, its own sigh of relief made a bubble in the guck. *It was fantastic!   The creatures all wanted to know how to blow bubbles in their guck. So the creature held a school to teach the other creatures how to blow bubbles in their guck.*

They renamed it Bubble Guck. They wanted to spread the good news. So they traveled around the solar system on their Guck Mobile until they crashed on Earth.

They told humans about Bubble Guck and humans made a new recipe, and they changed the name to gum, or Bubble Gum. The humans paid the creatures back with a year's supply of Bubble Gum.

Big Foot

It was a sultry spring evening. I had barely crawled into my sleeping bag when I heard a noise. It was coming from the bushes next to me.

My parents had already gone to sleep.   I was getting frightened, too frightened to get out of my sleeping bag. I tried to scoot over by our camper when suddenly, the noise got louder.   It sounded like chewing and chomping.

I jumped out of the sleeping bag and ran for the camper. When I got in the camper, I looked out the window, and Big Foot was out there eating my sleeping bag and flashlight,

and it was starting to eat our camper. *I went to wake my parents and they were gone! My sister and brother were gone too!*

I woke up in my own bedroom.

It was all a bad dream.

Christy and the Sea King

One sunny day in Illinois, a girl named Christy was swimming in her backyard pool when she saw birds with flowers in their beaks fly out of her pool.

And a frog hopped over beside her and said, "The prince is coming."

She thought that she was dreaming. A fat fish's head came out above the surface of the water. The frog bowed. The fish was a pretty, shiny, bluish-green.

It started to speak, and in a whisper, said, "Come with me, I won't harm you."

Christy thought for a minute and then followed the fish under the water.

Deeper and deeper they went. *She could breathe water!*

Suddenly her arms turned into wing-like things which made it easier for her to swim. She went a lot faster with the wings.

Her pool was not as deep as where they were going. The water got darker. They came to a giant seashell with fish swimming around it and singing a song.

The fish that she was following burped and the seashell opened.

It was all like a dream to her. There was a door made of diamonds and rubies. The fish did a handstand and the door opened.

Every fish and sea creature cheered and were so happy because the king was trapped in that room, and to get the door open, they had to have a human standing by it.

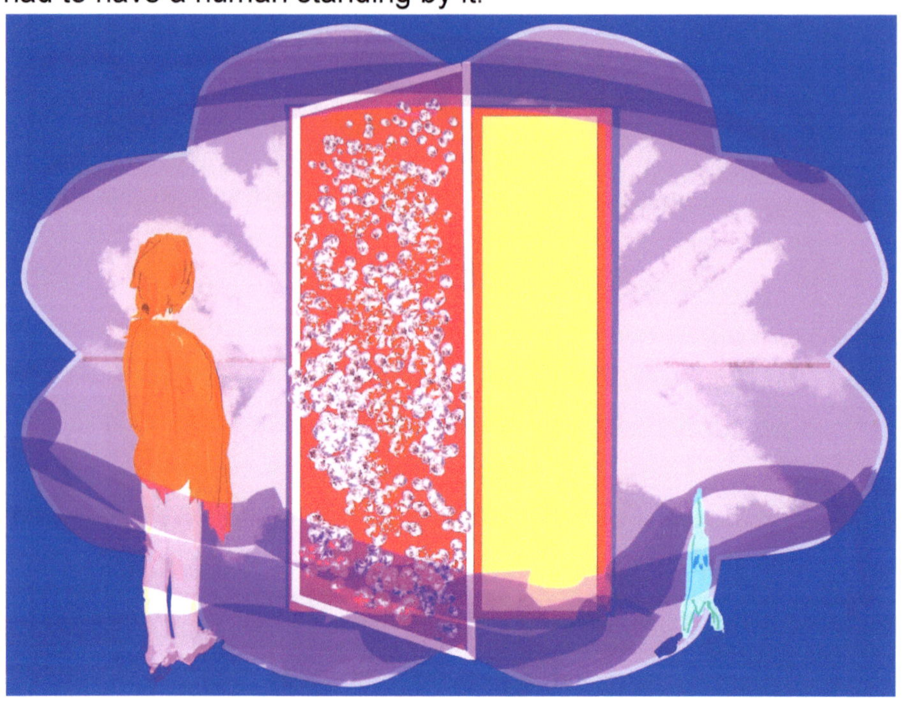

The king gave her a crown that was beautiful!

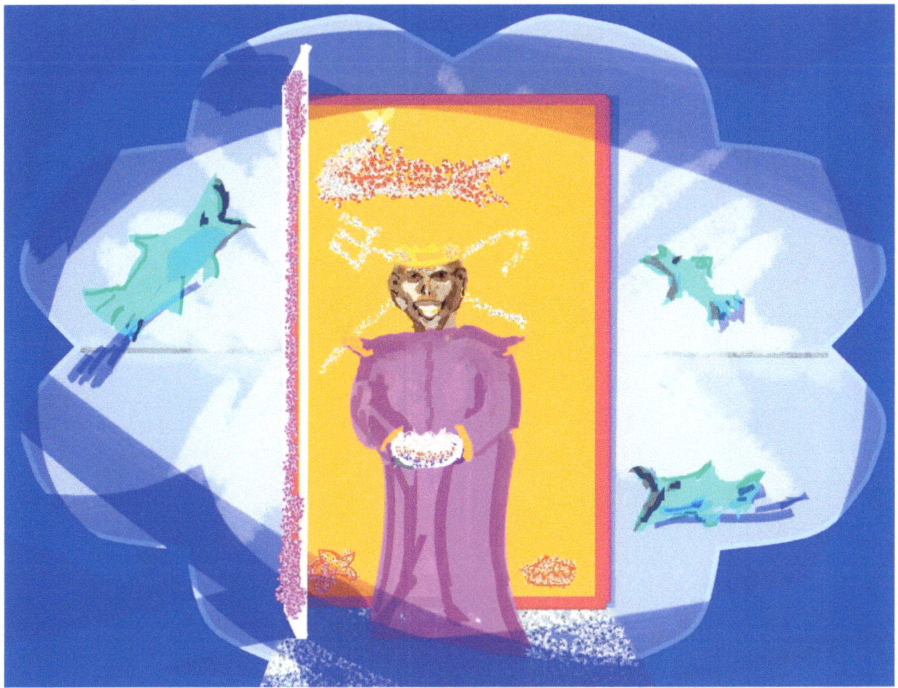

She put it on and then asked how she could get home. *A fish told her a secret way to go, and when she got out of the pool, it was exactly the same time of day, and her crown that was once coral*

and jewels, was rocks and dirt.

The Golden Pond

The silver gates around the golden pond were almost as beautiful as the pond itself. The flowers on the gate were colors and shapes that nobody had ever heard of or seen in the whole world.

Imagine another color that you have never seen in your life.

Well, the unicorns that drank at the pond had imagined a beautiful and graceful bird that they had never seen before.   One night Uni and Crystal, who were both unicorn friends, were looking at the stars, and they saw a rainbow come down from the moon and two swans come sliding down on it. One was white and one was black.

They slid right into the pond from the rainbow which stretched from the moon over the silver gate to the pond.

Uni and Crystal went over to the pond and watched the swans swim. When the morning came, both swans went under the water and hid.   Uni and Crystal told their parents about the swans, but when their parents came to see the swans in the daylight, they could not find them, so they did not believe what they had been told by Uni and Crystal.

Finally, one night the parents went to the pond and saw the swans swimming around.   Word spread quickly about the amazing, graceful birds in the golden pond, and all of the unicorns gathered at the pond and watched the swans in amazement.

They had never seen a swan before.

Another Ugly Face in the Crowd

Twelve-and-a-half-year-old Betsy Conder was in the middle of a math test when she started dreaming of being popular, famous, and special. Even though she was not any of those things, she imagined that she was. She finished taking her test and got an F, but still she was happy because she loved going to her imaginary world where she was a great skater, ice skater, gymnast, dancer, pianist, singer, and she was great at any talent that you could think of.

Because she didn't have any talent at all, her imaginary world was so special to her. She was shy and only had a few friends.

Laura and Jenny, with a crowd of girls, walked by her and said, "Give it up, your just another ugly face in the crowd," as Betsy was trying to do a back walk over.

Upset, Betsy sat down under the tree by her class and started to dream of her own world again. She walked into her world and people were cheering and applauding her. She realized that she was lonely in the real world.

She went to the ruler of her imaginary world, who was very nice and asked him what she should do. He told her, "Leave and never come back!"

She was shocked and sad because she loved the ruler and everyone in her imaginary world. She didn't want to leave, but she sadly agreed to go.

As she went to go, he said, "Remember us, but don't come back." As she said goodbye, she saw a tear come out of the ruler's eye.

He said, "We will miss you."

She heard the piercing sound of the bell, and as she ran to the classroom door, Patty and her started talking. Betsy would never forget her own world, but she just discovered a real and new one.

The Purple Submarine

Once upon a time, an old man didn't want to be old. He wished
he was still a kid. He wished and wished. As he was gazing out
his window, one night he saw a falling star. He wished upon the
star.

The next day he was fishing. When he threw out the hook, it
tugged and tugged, but the old man could not pull it in because he
was too weak. Instead he was pulled in by the tremendous
weight of whatever it was at the other end of the line.

He was pulled underwater and sucked into a strange purple
submarine that the hook was caught on. Inside the submarine, it
was blue. Nobody appeared to be in the submarine.

He went over to a room that had the controls and tried to work them.   The submarine started going out of control. He saw an orange submarine, a green submarine, and even a yellow one pass by the window.

A pink one crashed into him.

He heard a beep.

He went over to another room and saw a dragon.

The dragon said, "You wish to be young?"

The old man answered, "Yes I do, very much."

The dragon picked up the old man and brought him to a portal which he opened and threw the old man into the water and said,

"Have a good day."

The old man swam back up to the shore and saw that it was his own old fishing hole from when he was a kid. He looked at his hands and feet. *He was young again!*

Finnegan

One cold day in Alaska, a baby harp seal was born. His name was Finnegan. Happily, every day he would roll and play hide and seek in the snow with his friends.

His mother taught him new things almost every day. He was white and furry.

His mother was wise and always had sayings for things. One day he was crying because his best friend had died.

His mother hugged him and said, "Remember yesterday, dream of tomorrow, but live for today."

He didn't quite understand because he was so little.

One morning he was awakened by the sound of people. He didn't know what they were. His mom woke up and saw them. To Finnegan and his mother, the people looked like big, ugly creatures. The people came toward them.

They had clubs. The mother tried to protect Finnegan as best she could, but the people killed her.

With tears pouring from his eyes, Finnegan remembered a hiding place where none of his friends could find him when they played hide and seek.

He hid there. After a day or two, the people left. They had killed his friends and neighbors. He was alone and on his own. He was scared.

He heard the soft voice of his mother say, "Remember yesterday, dream of tomorrow, but live for today."

He wandered for miles. A day later he saw a lot of harp seals. They were all having a good time. *They saw him and asked him to live with them because they saw how sad he was.*

Point
Reyes